## About this Book

"Footprints on the Ceiling" is more than a story. It is also a keepsake you can treasure forever. Follow these easy directions to transform "Footprints on the Ceiling" into a book that is truly as unique as your child.

On the opposite page you will find an ink strip. It contains an ink formulated especially for making prints. It goes on evenly and washes with soap and water. (Disposable wet wipes work very well.) First remove the ink strip from the book. Next separate the two sheets of plastic to expose the ink. Set one sheet aside. Use the other to smear the ink onto your child's foot. Place his or her foot anywhere in the book as though your child were "walking" through the book. Repeat the process as many times as you wish. Discard the used half of the ink strip. Now use the other half of the ink strip to make a special "keepsake" footprint inside the frame on page 1. Be sure to keep "Footprints on the Ceiling" in a special place. You will want to enjoy this journey for many years to come.

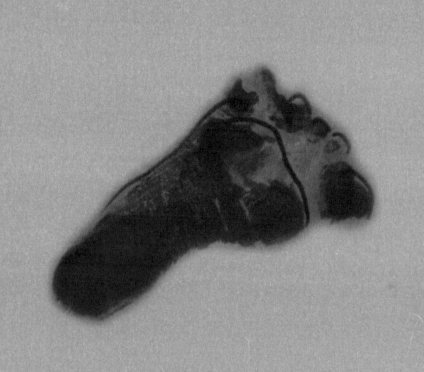

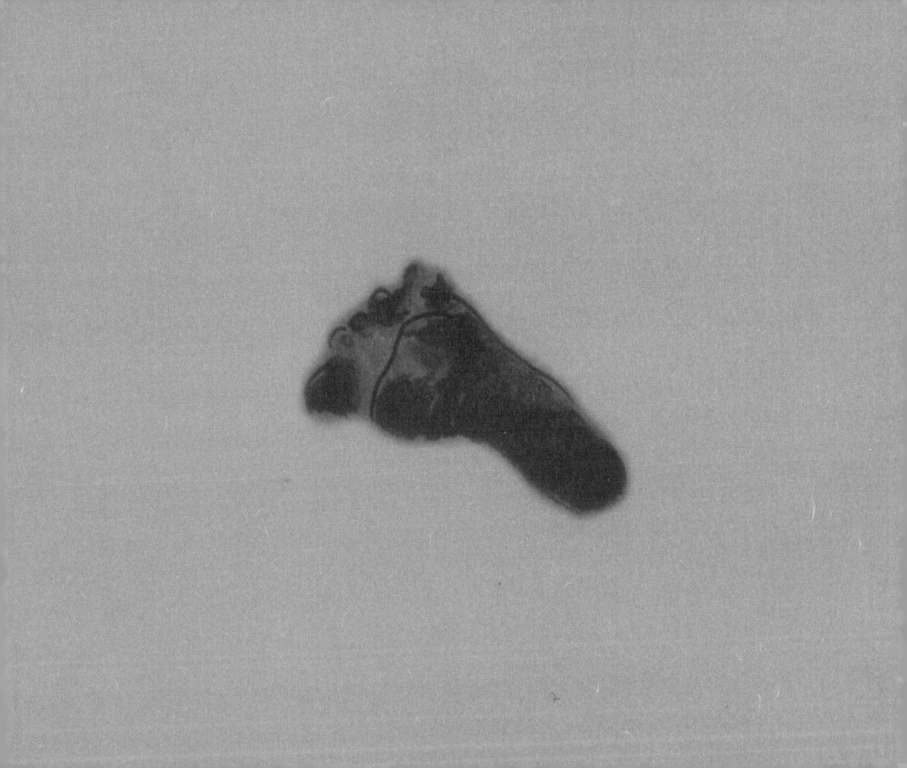

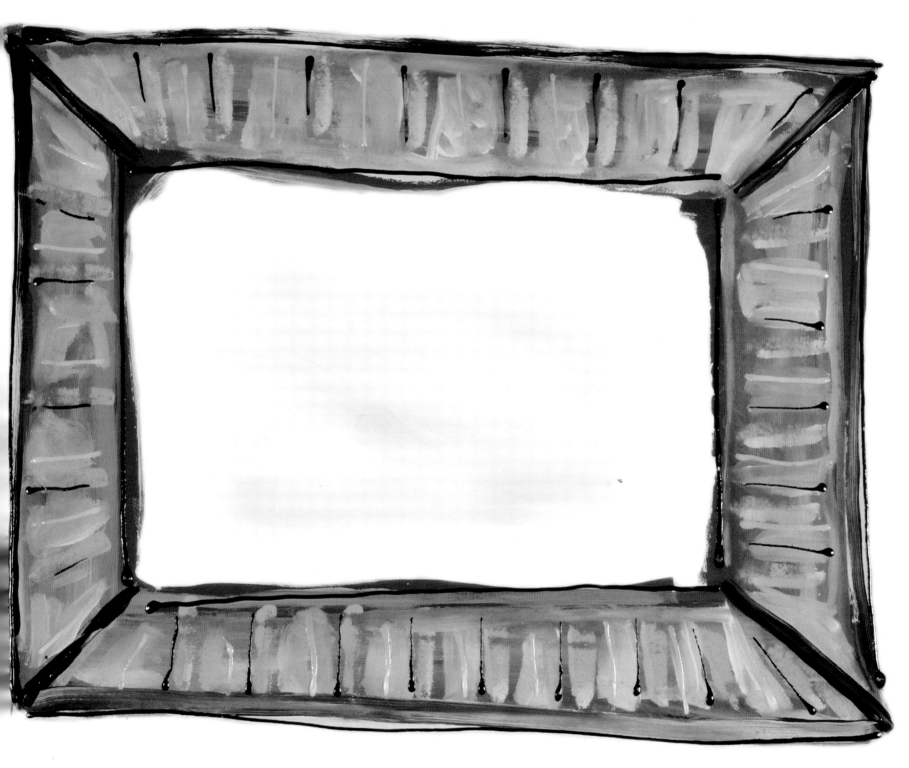

Webster Henrietta Publishing
P.O. Box 50044
Myrtle Beach, SC  29579
(843) 251-8867
www.websterhenrietta.com


Design by Shelley Powers

0-9728222-1-6 Collector's Edition
0-9728222-2-4 Second Edition

 Printed in Hong Kong

For information about this book and other products of Webster Henrietta Publishing, visit our website at www.websterhenrietta.com.

# Footprints on the Ceiling

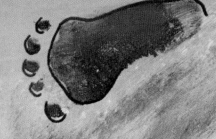

Michael Hetzer

Illustrated by Kim Clayton

WH
Webster Henrietta
Publishing

Haley Mae O'Theaming
Eight years old, yet seeming
Much older than her age.
Had upon her ceiling
A thing that strained believing.

But who looks at ceilings, anyway?
Sure, we look at floors to find our way.
We look at walls for pretty pictures.
But ceilings are bare and bumpy, gray.
All but hers, that is, the ceiling of Haley Mae.

For above her bed, to the right a wee pinch

By the window, there, you mustn't squinch.

Do you see what cannot, must not, should not,

No, not ever be? Try, it's a cinch.

You see them, don't you? Footprints.


Footprints! A baby's to be sure.

Marching to and fro, window to door

Black smudges of an upside-down baby walking.

In number, 27, no less, no more

Footprints no bigger than the leaf of a sycamore.

Poor Haley lay in bed each night

Counting them all by the dim night light

Dreading their meaning, certain it was bad

And her fear swelled and swelled right up to fright

Like the bump that rises after a mosquito bite.

For some strange reason she could never explain
The footprints stood as a message plain
From a father she missed and wished were here.
And a heaviness like clothes soaked by rain
Washed over her. How she wished just to see him again!

Which was why she asked her mom that week.
(Bottled up, the question came out as a shriek.)
"Why do I have footprints on my ceiling?"
Her mother froze; did not speak,
And a wet pearl, smooth and cold, kissed her cheek.

Haley did not ask again. Could not.

But the question wouldn't shrink, it grew, in fact—a lot.

She had to do something, and something's what she did.

She became a kid-detective in ponytail and sock

Detecting for clues like a modern-day Sherlock.

So many theories popped into her head.

She was the kind of girl who could make rope from thread,

Spinning great ideas from the smallest weave,

Baking great ideas, turning dough to bread.

"Anything is possible," was a thing Haley Mae often said.

Perhaps the house once stood upside-down

With rooftop aimed straight into the ground

And the people who lived there, did what seemed right

And walked on the ceiling as though it were ground

These upside-down folks, who knew not up from down.

Perhaps it was an angel baby, a child a-wing

Who trip-tropped each night on Haley's ceiling

An angel who could, with a single flip-flap,

Rise up from the floor to play, dance, sing

Invisibly, of course, out of sight of eyes seeing.

Perhaps the child was in fact a ghost

Who died tragically while walking the sea coast

Leaving footprints in the sand, now repeated

On Haley's ceiling each night as a child's boast:

"I died, yes, but in the place I love most."

Perhaps it was a baby put together not right
With legs eight-feet long—not the normal-size height.
Or a crib, perhaps, with springs that sprang too high
So many theories, but only one was right
Haley Mae had to know which to cure her night fright.

So she shifted her dresser; got up on a chair

And craned her neck way up high in the air

For a close-up inspection of the mysterious prints

She measured their length, brushed back her hair

Then consulted a baby-foot-growth chart to compare.


The child, she concluded, was aged about two.

But who? How many? One? A few?

So she got out a pencil and sketched the smudgy toe,

And compared it to hers, after removing her shoe.

The prints were her own...

But somehow, she already knew.

"Why are you crying?" Mother asked her with dread.

After coming upstairs to find Haley's eyes burning red.

Haley sniffled, "I remembered something, Mama, something…"

"What?" Mama urged, now sitting on the bed.

"Something… not a dream," Haley said.


"I see a man's face upside-down.

"He's laughing, though I can't hear a sound.

"His arms are outstretched. It's me he's holding

"While I walk from window to door, all around.

"On the bumpy ceiling as if it were bumpy ground."

"The bumps," said Mama after a pause, "tickled your toes."

She nodded, and Haley saw sadness in her repose.

"So he held you aloft, his strong arms aching.

"It was the day he left, the day that I chose

"Not to clean them, the footprints; of them, I could not dispose."


And Mama held Haley; Mama half-leaning

And they stayed like that till the house needed cleaning.

And from that day forward Haley slept soundly in her room.

Her father's love was no more just a vague thing seeming.

It was real. Palpable. Powerful. Protecting.

His love was a promise through space and time reaching

His love *was* the footprints upon her ceiling.

**Michael Hetzer** is the author of numerous books, including "No More Handprints," (Webster Henrietta Publishing) and "The Forbidden Zone," (Simon & Schuster). He is also the founding editor of "The Moscow Times," the first English-language daily newspaper in Russia. Hetzer lives in Myrtle Beach, South Carolina with his wife, Tamara, and their children, Stephanie and Conrad.

**Kim Clayton** collaborated with Hetzer on his previous children's book, "No More Handprints." She is an internationally-known folk artist, whose paint brush never touches canvas; she paints only on trash and dubs her method, "trash to treasure." Clayton lives in Myrtle Beach, South Carolina with her husband David and their three children, Leslie, David and Noah. It is Kim's prayer that every child who reads this book can know the love of the Father above.

*From Michael Hetzer*
For Stephanie and Conrad, my oh-so-wise teachers.


*From Kim Clayton*
For my dear friend, Brandy Tankersley. Remember, a father's love cannot die.